KING FLASHYPANTS

AND THE Creature from Crong

BOOK 2

WRITTEN AND DRAWN BY **ANDY RILEY**

Henry Holt and Company · New York

Henry Holt and Company, *Publishers since 1866*
Henry Holt® is a registered trademark of Macmillan Publishing Group, LLC
175 Fifth Avenue, New York, New York 10010 • mackids.com

ISBN 978-1-62779-811-2
Library of Congress Control Number 2017945042

Our books may be purchased in bulk for promotional, educational, or business
use. Please contact your local bookseller or the Macmillan Corporate and
Premium Sales Department at (800) 221-7945 ext. 5442 or by e-mail at
MacmillanSpecialMarkets@macmillan.com.

Originally published in 2017 in Great Britain by Hodder and Stoughton
First American edition, 2018 / Design by Jennifer Stephenson
Printed in the United States of America by LSC Communications,
Harrisonburg, Virginia

1 3 5 7 9 10 8 6 4 2

With thanks to

Polly Faber, Eddie Riley, Bill Riley,

Emma Goldhawk, Jennifer Stephenson,

Anne McNeil, Gordon Wise,

Hilary Murray Hill, Lucy Upton,

Fritha Lindqvist, Stephanie Allen,

Kevin Cecil, and Tim Robinson

Dedicated to

Greta Riley and Robin Riley

and also to

ALL THE LIBRARIANS

EMPEROR NURBISON

GLOBULUS

BAXTER

COLIN

The Names of ALL THE GRIPPING CHAPTERS You're About to Read

They're Good for You

The boy pushed a pile of vegetables around on his plate. He wasn't an ordinary boy. He was a king. King Edwin Flashypants the First. There wasn't a King Edwin Flashypants the Second or Third yet, but everybody in Edwin's little kingdom thought

it was such a great name that there were bound to be loads more kings called Edwin Flashypants in the future.

But even though the boy was special, the vegetables were very, very ordinary. There was cabbage, and spinach, and something that drooped like the nose of an old witch when Edwin picked it up with his fork. It had witchy pimples, too, and it dripped green water that looked a bit like snot.

So why was this king, who had suits of armor and a big shiny crown and a castle with its own bowling alley, eating a plate full of food he didn't like?

King Edwin couldn't do everything he wanted to. Being a king is hard—you've got to look after a whole kingdom-load of people. Imagine doing that when you're just nine years old. So Edwin needed a grown-up to help him rule Edwinland, and her name was Minister Jill.

A month or two before this very vegetable-ish lunch, Minister Jill decided people in Edwinland were eating too many treats.

> PEOPLE IN EDWINLAND ARE EATING TOO MANY TREATS.

That's what she said.

So she made the candy shops open for just two hours a day instead of twenty-four. She had the peasants digging huge vegetable patches next to Village, which was the name of the only village in Edwinland. Then she put up posters saying:

Minister Jill was just trying to keep everyone healthy, like a good minister should. But nobody seemed to be saying "Wow, thanks, Jill!"

Today, just for once, Jill wasn't standing behind Edwin as he chewed slimy vegetables in the castle's banqueting hall. She had taken the afternoon off work to do that thing grown-ups do sometimes, when they "pamper" themselves and have some "me time." These were the days when Jill would listen to calming music and get her feet massaged, all while worrying about what trouble Edwin might get into next.

Edwin wasn't alone, though. His best friend, Megan the Jester, ate beside him. She liked piles of vegetables even less than he

did, so she was finding ways to get them
off her plate without actually eating them.
Megan tucked zucchini into the pointy bits
of her jester hat. Then she pushed broccoli
through the strings of her lute. It didn't make
much difference. There were still tons more
to munch through.

"Help! Help!" A panicked voice
floated through the banqueting hall's window
and right into King Edwin's ear.

Edwin pushed his plate away and stood up.

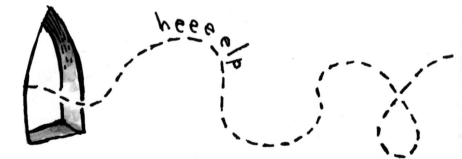

"Megan? Somebody needs our help, and I'm fairly sure about that because he said 'help' twice. Let's go!"

It was also a great excuse to stop eating the vegetables, but Edwin didn't say that out loud.

"Your Majesty!" said Megan. "Helping people in need is so splendidly kingly!"

After she had applauded the king for five whole minutes, they ran outside to see what all the fuss was about.

By now the man who had shouted "Help!"
was running around the streets of Village.
His name was Baxter, and nobody had seen
him for years because he was a hermit.
He lived all by himself in the Wilderness of
Crong, in a hut made from dead wasps.

Being a hermit can be lonely—but on the other hand, there's no one around to nag you about washing your armpits.

Baxter was famous for his beard, which was so long and bushy it covered his whole body. Nobody was ever sure if he was wearing clothes underneath or not, and everybody was too embarrassed to ask.

"What's the matter, Mr. Sir Gentleman Fellow Good Sir?" said Edwin. The king always wanted to be polite, but he couldn't remember exactly which words to use, so he used all the ones he knew.

"There's-a-monster-and-it's-eating-everything-oh-no-the-monster-the-monster-oh-no!" Baxter gabbled.

"Please, slow down a bit," said Edwin.

"*Theeeerrrrreeee'sss aaaaaa mooooonssstteerr...*"

"Okay, a bit faster than that," said Edwin. "Kind of medium speed."

"There's a monster, young man!" said Baxter. "In the Wilderness of Crong. We thought it dead these last hundred years, but we were mistaken. Turns out, it was just having a long nap. And now it's awake, and oh, it's the most terrifying thing!"

Baxter was shaking and his eyes were bulging. It really was something to see. Peasants came running just to watch.

"It's taller than a quite tall man standing on a box!" Baxter spluttered. "Its teeth are longer and sharper than bread knives! It has seven eyes! It ate all my goats and then gobbled up my best cow in one gulp, it did, it did! They say it can eat people, too!"

"What's it called?" asked Megan.

"Its name? I shall tell you.

Its name . . .

its name . . .

its name . . .

its name . . ."

I like dramatic pauses as much as the *next boy,* thought Edwin, *but I hope he gets* *to it soon.*

Edwin thought about all those poor

people beyond his merry kingdom, frightened

for their lives with this Voolith running about.

Then he thought about how he had to eat what he was told, like a little boy. Edwin wanted to be just like a grown-up king, and do all the brave and bold things grown-up kings do.

King Edwin Flashypants took a deep breath and spoke to the crowd.

"People of Edwinland! The good folk of Crong need my help. And they'll get it! I will cross the wilderness and fight the Voolith!"

Megan and the peasants cheered and threw their hats in the air. Those who didn't have hats ran to buy them from the hat shop, just so they could throw them in the air, too.

"A proper king always keeps his promises. And I promise you this—I will defeat the Voolith, in single combat!"

"Our king is so brave!" said one peasant.

"He is a powerful force for good in this world!" said another.

Then Edwin realized he didn't know what *single combat* meant, exactly. But he was fairly sure it involved some big metal box with spiky wheels, and a big boxing glove on the front that punches monsters while you relax inside it and drink lemonade.

The Windmill of Nightmares

Next to a crashing gray sea, a man was talking to a golf ball. It wasn't the first time he'd done this. But because he was Emperor Nurbison of Nurbisonia, the most evil ruler the world had ever seen, nobody dared say it was a silly thing to do.

The emperor had been thinking about Edwinland all morning, and that made him angry. He hated Edwinland because it didn't belong to him, and because King Edwin made it a land of friendship and joy. Friendship and joy were another two things Emperor Nurbison didn't like.

When he got too angry, he played mini golf to relax. But he relaxed in quite a shouty way.

"Hear me, feeble golf ball! My skill upon the mini-golf course is legend across the earth! Globulus? Fetch me . . .

THE CLUB OF CHAOS."

Globulus, the emperor's tiny, loyal,
beach-ball-shaped helper, came running
with the Club of Chaos. It truly was a golf
club fit for a terrifying ruler. Instead of a
flange of metal on the end, it had a gleaming
silver skull, with a sticky-out jawbone for
hitting the ball.

Everything Emperor Nurbison owned was as spiky and frightening as he could make it. His castle was a tall mass of jagged stone with bats living everywhere inside it—even under the toilet seats.

His crown was so dark and spooky
that some said it was haunted by a chain-
dragging ghost called Clanky Peter.

The emperor steadied himself and took
his stroke.

WHACK.

He hit the ball much too hard.

It went FLUMPH! into the long grass.

"Doesn't count! You threw me off, Globulus. I'm taking it again."

It was the emperor's private mini-golf course, so the emperor made the rules.

When Nurbison finally got the ball into the hole, he filled in his scorecard. *Don't like the look of this*, he thought.

Even though Nurbison had been cheating the numbers since the second hole, Globulus would still win.

There was just one hole left to play. The windmill.

"My favorite hole!" said the emperor, very loudly, because he knew he was always really bad at this one. You had to get the ball straight through a narrow tunnel, missing the spinning windmill sails. It was super hard.

He was starting to hate the windmill almost as much as he hated King Edwin— and he really, really hated King Edwin, so that was saying something.

The emperor went first. Twenty-seven thwacks later, his ball was in the hole. Now for Globulus.

Globulus walloped his ball. It pinged off a DON'T WALK ON THE GRASS sign, boinged off Globulus's nose, then rattled through the tunnel. Emperor Nurbison and Globulus heard the unmistakable PLOP of a hole in one.

"Wait there!" snapped the emperor.

The emperor
walked behind
the windmill. There
was Globulus's
ball, sitting in
the hole.

The
emperor
peeped
back around the
windmill to check
that Globulus
was out of
sight.

He
dug a
pointy boot

into the hole, wiggled out the little white ball, and kicked it as hard as he could. It sailed through the air and splashed into the sea.

"Oh no, Globulus! An unlucky bounce sent your ball into the sea. So now it's lost . . . Emperor Nurbison wins yet again!

FOO HOO HOO HOO!"

This was Emperor Nurbison's evil laugh, chosen because it was the most chilling, terrifying sound in all the world.

"Want a trophy, give me a trophy now," said the emperor.

Globulus handed Nurbison a shining gold cup with WORLD'S BEST GOLFER engraved on it. The emperor waved it around like a champion. Five seconds later, he was bored.

"Where's my golf cart?" he said.

"Here, Your Greatness," said a thin man.

The emperor sat on the thin man's back, and the man crawled along a muddy path, all the way back to the evil castle.

The thin man was one of hundreds who had run from the Wilderness of Crong in the last couple of days, fleeing this "Voolith" creature.

At first, Emperor Nurbison sent his sinister soldiers to stop people from getting into Nurbisonia, because that was a mean thing to do, and doing mean things was the emperor's favorite hobby.

Then he realized he was missing a trick. If he let them in, he would have hundreds more people to be nasty to every day. So in they came, and the emperor gave them all rotten jobs to do.

The emperor heaved open the door
to his castle's trophy room. The room was
crammed so high with shiny cups, shields,
and statuettes that dozens of them tumbled
onto his head.

He threw his new mini-golf cup on
the top of the pile, and with the help of
Globulus (and a lot of clanging),
he just about managed to close
the door again.

Then he sat back on his throne and put his boots up on a Crong peasant he liked to call "Footrest."

That monster out in the wilderness must be really awful, thought the emperor, *if these Crong people think working for me is better than being out there. Yes, a fearsome monster indeed.*

A sinister soldier ran into the room.

"News from abroad, Your Greatness. King Edwin Flashypants says he'll go to the Wilderness of Crong and fight the Voolith."

Emperor Nurbison had a very long and deep think.

Then his face split into a villainous smile.

"Globulus! You know how very good I am at having **WICKED PLANS?**"

"Uhh, yeah, Your Brilliantness, definitely."

"Well, I've just had *two* of them," said the emperor. "One plan for Edwin Flashypants, and one for the monster. And they're such sly and dastardly schemes that I may need an extra tower to fit all the trophies for evilness I'll give myself afterward. When my first plan is complete—no more Edwin! And when my second is complete . . ."

"Ummm—no more monster?" said Globulus.

"No more Edwinland!" said the emperor. "Foo hoo hoo hoo! But I must prepare. Meet me in the Room of Old Maps. Bring paints, ink, and a wet tea bag. Oh, and mind your fingers, because I'm going to slam this door behind me so hard it'll blow all the candles out. Love doing that. Don't know why."

Nurbison slammed the door.

And Globulus couldn't find the tea bags,
because everything had just gone very dark.

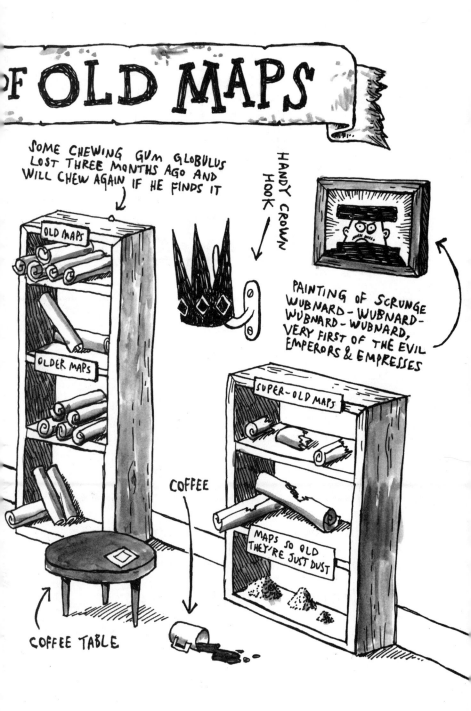

A Warrior Prepares

Minister Jill was pacing back and forth in King Edwin's throne room. She reminded Edwin of a rubber ball bouncing off the walls.

I lost my best rubber ball a week ago, thought Edwin. *I should tell everyone to look out for it. It's white, and I've bounced it so much it's covered in craters, like the moon.*

Then he thought:

? ? ? ?

I wonder if it's always the **same moon** ?

that crosses the sky,

or if a **fresh one**

comes over **every night?**

Maybe there's a

big

glowing pile of them

on the **other side** of the mountains.

And what are **moons made of**, anyway . . .

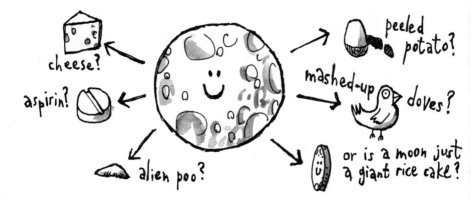

cheese?

aspirin?

alien poo?

peeled potato?

mashed-up doves?

or is a moon just a giant rice cake?

"Your Majesty! Please pay attention," said Minister Jill. "Do you actually know what *single combat* means?"

Edwin nodded.

Jill kept looking at him.

Edwin shook his head.

"It means that you, King Edwin Flashypants, have to fight this enormous monster all by yourself. With just a sword and a shield and nothing else."

Gulp, thought Edwin.

"Let's check the facts again," said Jill. "Please summon Baxter the Hermit!"

Megan the Jester pulled a piece of string attached to a wheel attached to another piece of string attached to a cog, and so on.

One minute later, Baxter plunked out of a chute.

Edwin's castle had loads of chutes and slides to get from room to room.

KINGS   HERMITS   JESTERS

"Mr. Baxter. Tell us again about this Voolith," said Jill.

"Its teeth are longer and sharper than pirates' swords!" said Baxter, shuddering. "It's got **sixty** eyes! And it's taller than a giraffe wearing two top hats at the same time!"

"Is it really so frightening?" asked Minister Jill. "I don't want to be rude, but I try not to believe everything cranky old hermits say."

Baxter delved into his bushy beard and pulled out a card.

MEMBERSHIP NUMBER: 90722

HERMIT HONESTY CARD

THE HOLDER OF THIS CARD Baxter the Hermit IS AN OFFICIAL MEMBER OF THE UNION OF HONEST HERMITS, AND NEVER LIES, FIBS, OR EXAGGERATES.

SIGNED,
The Chief Hermit

Megan wondered if Baxter had said "sixty eyes" last time, or some other number. But she decided not to say anything.

"We'll get you out of this, Your Majesty," said Jill. "We'll just say that while I had my afternoon off, you got a bit confused.

You can stay in the castle and play Hungry Hungry Griffins with Megan. Alisha and the palace guards will deal with the creature."

Centurion Alisha, the leader of Edwin's palace guards, saluted with both arms and one leg. She was so tough she could crack hazelnuts with her nostrils, and if she so much as looked at a tight jam jar lid, it would be so afraid of her powerful grip it would pop off the jar all by itself. If you could pick anyone to stop a giant monster, you would pick Alisha.

"No!" said Edwin, taking a kingly step forward, tripping over Megan's foot, then standing up again as if nothing had happened. "I promised to defeat the monster in single combat. And a proper king keeps his promises."

Jill couldn't argue with that.

• • •

Edwin would be gone hunting the Voolith for a few days, so he went to the castle kitchen to pack some food.

I know I should take nice healthy vegetables, thought Edwin, *but when you're doing something super brave like fighting off a monster, you deserve a few treats.* So he raided the Royal Candy Jar.

All kings have big candy jars. Boy kings have the very biggest. Edwin climbed a ladder up the side of his, then dived in. It was like jumping into a ball pit. A delicious, sugary ball pit. He filled a big sack with jawbreakers, chocolate wafers, peanut caramel bars, and chewy red licorice twists.

The Wilderness of Crong is big, thought Edwin. *Better take a little bit more.*

"More sacks, please!" the king called.

Edwin's next job was to gather companions for his quest.

Megan was his first pick. Singing songs is a big part of a jester's job, and Megan wanted to write a really exciting one, telling the story of their adventure. So she packed musical instruments.

A LUTE

A PIANJO

A TROMBO-XYLO-SAXOPHONE

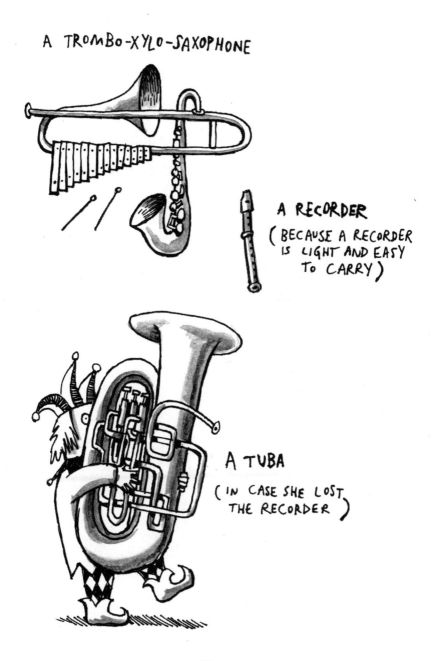

A RECORDER
(BECAUSE A RECORDER
IS LIGHT AND EASY
TO CARRY)

A TUBA
(IN CASE SHE LOST
THE RECORDER)

Jill would come, too. Edwin might be a brave king on a quest, but he knew he needed someone to remind him to brush his teeth.

The fourth member of the team would be Colin. He was Edwin's pony, given to Edwin when the king was five. The king had grown since then. Colin hadn't.

Half the peasants in the kingdom
came to see the friends leave, because they
loved their king and because it made a nice
change from growing lettuce.

The crowd gave Edwin a huge cheer. He
looked so dashing in his shiny armor.

"If I were a different
sort of boy, this
might make me
bigheaded,"
said Edwin
to Jill as he
waved to all
the girls and
unfurled a big
flag with his
own face on it.

"Neigh," said Colin, because he was just a horse.

King Edwin hopped onto Colin and rode over the dotted line that marked the edge of Edwinland and into the Plains of Yerm. The adventure had begun.

Five seconds later, Edwin's path was blocked by a huge horse's leg covered in shimmering black hair.

Just as he suspected, the leg was attached to an entire horse. And on the horse, in a black suit of armor, was Edwin's worst enemy.

"KING EDWIN FLASHYPANTS? I CHALLENGE YOU TO A JOUST!" said Emperor Nurbison.

The Joust

The emperor leaped off his horse and strode in front of the crowd. His black armor glinted magnificently in the sun, but it hadn't been oiled for ages, so it made horrible squealing noises that hurt everybody's ears.

Globulus ran after the emperor, squirting blobs of oil from a can.

"I am Emperor Nurbison, Earl of Unjerland, Overlord of Glenth and Boolander, and lots of other places listed on the helpful fact sheet that Globulus will give you. Now hear this!"

SQUEEEK SQUEAAAA SQUEEEE SQWARR

"The poor, innocent people of Crong
have suffered too long from this
fearsome Voolith. We've all heard how
dreadful and scary it is."

"They say it has **one hundred and fifty-three** eyes!" wailed Baxter.

The peasants gasped. This monster must be growing new eyes all the time.

"The people of Crong need a hero to save them from the Voolith. Emperor Nurbison is that hero!" said Emperor Nurbison.

Nurbison drew his sword and posed like a statue. Sinister soldiers blew a trumpet fanfare. The emperor knew how to put on a show.

"Yet puny king Edwin, who is so puny, claims his puny sword will defeat the beast," said the emperor.

While he was working away in his Room of Old Maps, the emperor had noticed a book called *Cool Words for Evil Rulers to Use*. That morning, he had read the page about *puny*.

"We cannot both fight this monster in single combat. So we shall joust! As always, the winner shall claim a prize from the loser—but he shall also have the honor of hunting the mighty Voolith! What say you, puny Edwin of Punyland?"

"You shouldn't do things just because he wants you to," whispered Minister Jill to Edwin.

"He's just a big bully," said Megan the Jester.

"Oh, we all know what he's like," said Edwin. "But if I can't beat him, I can't beat a great big monster, can I? Yes. This'll be good practice for me."

The joust was on.

Jousting is an olden-days sport where two people on horses gallop at each other, holding lances. *Lance* is just a fancy word for "long stick." Whoever knocks the other one off their horse is the winner, and the loser has to give the winner a prize.

It's great fun, but very dangerous, so don't try it unless you live in the olden days.

Colin didn't look like anyone's idea of a jousting horse. When people saw him, they usually thought, *Wow, that's a very realistic-looking toy horse*. And Edwin's lance was the smallest size from the "Junior Dragonslayer" department at the local Knights Direct shop.

Emperor Nurbison mounted his magnificent charger. Sinister soldiers came running with the emperor's lance. It was the longest anyone had ever seen—as long as ten horses. It was so very, very long it had a few sets of wheels to help the emperor hold it up.

The soldiers clamped a huge helmet onto Nurbison's head.

"Let the joust begin!" said the emperor, but because his voice was echoing in the helmet, it sounded more like:

Everyone could guess what he meant, more or less.

King Edwin and Emperor Nurbison took their positions.

And charged.

Jill and Megan could barely watch. How would Edwin knock the emperor off his horse when Nurbison's lance was sure to hit him first?

As the tip of the Evil Emperor's lance approached, Edwin whispered in Colin's ear.

"One, two, three . . . jump!"

The tiny horse jumped—and a moment later, it was galloping along the top of the emperor's lance.

The emperor galloped on. With his bucket of a helmet, he couldn't see a thing.

King Edwin tickled the emperor under his armpit.

"YOWWWAHH-HHAA-HHAA!"

cried Emperor Nurbison, jumping out of his saddle and tumbling to the ground with a great clanging

Moments later, King Edwin was still sitting on his horse.

Which was standing on the big black horse.

And Nurbison was wriggling in the mud.

"GRRRRGGGRRGGR!" said the emperor.

"Errmmm—sorry, Your Greatness, couldn't quite, y'know, hear that through the helmet," said Globulus.

"GRRRRGGGRRGGR!"

"I think he's saying *Take my helmet off*," said Minister Jill.

"Is she right, Your Greatness? Tell me if she is," said Globulus.

"GGRRGRRRGRRRRR—GRR! GGRGRRRGRRGRR!"

Globulus took the emperor's helmet off.

"King Edwin Flashypants, you won the joust fair and square. You shall fight the Voolith," said Nurbison calmly. "But first, you must claim a prize from me."

Normally Emperor Nurbison absolutely hates to lose, thought Edwin. *But he's being very good about it this time. Makes a nice change.*

Nurbison unbuckled his big saddlebag and sifted through it.

"Let's see . . . my spooky drinking cup shaped like a vampire's head . . . a map of the Wilderness of Crong, but you probably won't want that . . . a jar of my belly-button fluff . . ."

"Stop!" said King Edwin. "The map of the Wilderness of Crong! I haven't got one of those, and it's bound to come in handy. I'll have that, thank you."

"Neigh," said Colin, because he was just a horse.

The emperor handed Edwin the map.

As Edwin rode away, he couldn't be happier. The joust had turned out great. Yes, this adventure was going to be fun all the way, and by the end, everyone would know he was a proper king. Nothing would mess that up now.

As King Edwin glanced back at the emperor,

he thought—for just one second—that he saw Nurbison smile an evil smile.

And stroke his evil beard.

And pump his evil fist.

No, must be imagining it, thought Edwin.

There was another thought Edwin didn't have—but maybe he should have.

Did Emperor Nurbison lose the joust on purpose?

Into the Wilderness

The four adventurers journeyed all day over the Plains of Yerm. Colin soon got tired of carrying King Edwin—so before the end of the day, Megan was carrying Colin as well as all the baggage.

As the sun dipped in the sky, somehow
Edwin and his friends knew they were
entering the Wilderness of Crong. Perhaps it
was the cold edge to the wind, or the swaying
of the bushes. Or maybe it was the Day-Glo
orange sign as big as a house that said:

YOU ARE NOW
ENTERING THE
WILDERNESS
OF CRONG

"Let's camp for the night," said the
minister.

Jill unpacked a tiny stove and gathered
wood to light inside it. Soon she had a
bubbling pot of water, ready to cook dinner.

"What shall we have?" said Jill. "I
thought kale or parsnips. Maybe cauliflower
for a bit of a treat."

She glanced at King Edwin and Megan
the Jester, who were both shoving their hands
into big bags of candy.

Minister Jill scrunched up her eyes and
pressed two fingers against her forehead.

Edwin thought he knew all the little moves Jill did when she was stressed, but he hadn't seen this one before, and he reminded himself to add it to the list.

"Did you just bring candy?" said Jill. "No vegetables at all?"

Megan rummaged in her bag and pulled out a green gummy worm.

"Sorry, Megan. A gummy worm is not a vegetable," said Jill.

"But it's green," said Megan.

"It's made of sugar, starch, and corn syrup," said Jill.

"But it's green," said Megan.

So Jill ate her green things, Megan ate her different green things, and Edwin ate mostly blue, purple, and stripy red things.

After dinner it was time to bed down for the night. The friends lay in their sleeping bags and gazed up at the stars. They were inside a tent, but Edwin's lance had ripped holes in it while Megan was carrying everything.

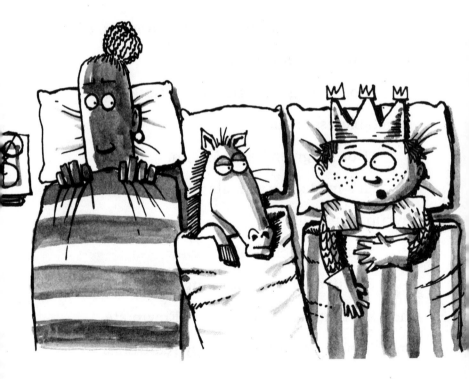

"I'm a bit worried about this adventure," said Edwin.

"Good," said Minister Jill. "If you're worried, that means you understand how dangerous it is."

"No, I mean, I'm worried it's all going to be too easy," said Edwin.

"With this map, we'll find the Voolith in no time."

At the top of the emperor's map of Crong, there was a place marked VOOLITH'S LAIR.

That was going to make monster hunting

a breeze. And the map couldn't be wrong,

because it was old and crinkly and brown,

and Edwin knew that old maps were the

wisest.

"And the joust proved I'm so good at

fighting that I'll beat the monster in a flash,"

Edwin continued.

"Yes. How can I write lots of verses for

my heroic song if the adventure is over all
too quickly?" said Megan. "We should think
of ways to make it harder and riskier. That's
the sensible thing to do."

"Neigh," said Colin, because he was just
a horse.

Then a rain cloud passed over, and
everybody in the tent got wet. Still, it gave
Megan something to write a verse about.

Slight dampness!

The king did suffer

slight dampness!

Which moistened

his ears

And chilled his chin

And drizzled the bag

He keeps underwear in.

They say only true

heroes do fight

Slight dampness.

The next day they trudged deeper and deeper into the barren wastes of Crong. On they went, all through Wednesday and Tuesday, following the emperor's map. Wednesday came before Tuesday because Crong was a wild place where even the days of the week didn't care about the rules.

On Thursday, the map said they were nearly at the Voolith's lair.

"We're nearly at the Voolith's lair," said Megan, because the map couldn't actually say it out loud, it being a piece of paper.

"Something's odd, though," said Jill. "If we're so close to its lair, why are there no Voolith footprints around?"

Minister Jill's so clever, thought Edwin. *She notices all kinds of things. Like that time I lost my toast and jam, and I looked for ages, until Jill told me it was stuck to my bottom.*

"I be a hermit! Yes, I be!" said a hermit, crawling out from under a stone and hobbling toward them. His walking stick was so wonky and twisty that it was a wonder it found the ground at all. His back was super-duper hunched. His nose was like five normal noses having a fight inside a sock.

This hermit was even more hermitish than Baxter.

"Greetings!" said King Edwin. "I've found I can normally trust everything hermits tell me. Seen the Voolith around?"

"Aye! I do seen that there Voolith. Horrific beastie! Taller than a tall tree that's wearing high heels! Teeth sharper than a bee's bum and longer than a wet Tuesday in the school holidays! And it has nine hundred and twenty-seven and a half eyes!"

"Hmmm. Its eyes must be breeding and having eye babies," said Minister Jill. "Hermit—are we going the right way?"

"Aye, that you be!" The hermit extended a trembling finger to the north. The path ahead was cloaked in mist. "Don't turn back now, young man! Face the Voolith! For you promised, so you did, and a king who does not keep his promises AIN'T NO KIND OF PROPER KING AT ALL!"

That was all Edwin needed to hear. On he marched, with his friends following after.

When they were definitely gone, the hermit straightened up and pulled off his fake nose.

"You can come out now, Globulus," said the emperor.

Globulus tumbled out of the filthy robes. He had been the hermit's hunch.

And Emperor Nurbison threw back his head, just as he was taught years ago in the Advanced Laughing Module at Evil School.

"FOO HOO HOO HOO HOO HOO HOO!"

Toads!

King Edwin Flashypants, Minister Jill, Colin the horse, and Megan the Jester stumbled through the mist.

"It's such a thick mist that I'd say it's more of a fog," said Minister Jill.

"Oh, but I think it's a mist. Can we say mist?" said Megan.

"But it's a fog," said Jill.

"Not a mist then?" said Megan.

"Let's not argue about it," said Minister Jill. "Why don't we say it's a bit of both? Part fog, part mist."

Megan said, "Definitely a bit of both. A sort of a . . . mig."

"Or a fost," said Minister Jill.

Edwin didn't care if they called it a mist or a fog or a mig or a fost or a mog or a fist, because it was surely made of steam

from the Voolith's breath. And he could hear
a rumbling noise up ahead, which was bound
to be coming from the creature's great tummy.
He checked the map one last time. Yes: the
Voolith's lair was right here.

"Quick! My sword, my shield!" said Edwin.

Megan threw him both, and Edwin caught
them in midair like real heroes do.

They had been practicing that move for
the last five days.

With his best friends by his side, his sword held high, and his shield held at a sort of medium height, Edwin ran hard up the hill, roaring his battle cry. He'd been practicing that, too.

As he was charging and roaring and whirling his sword all about, Edwin had a think. He thought: *This mist is so thick now, I can't see the ground below me.*

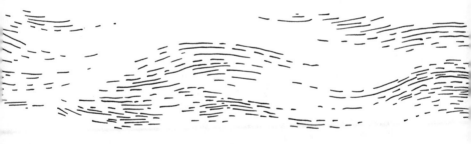

And it's suddenly very windy, and the wind is coming up from underneath. Wind doesn't do that often.

Oh yes, I see the problem, he thought. *We just ran over the edge of a cliff. That was a clever deduction. I should become a detective one day. But maybe right now I should scream a bit.*

"Neigh," said Colin, because he was just a horse.

"WHHEEEEEEE!!!" shouted Megan, just before she realized how much danger she was in.

"AAAAAHHHHHH!" shouted Minister Jill.

"AAAAAHHHHHHH!" shouted King Edwin.

Luckily their fall was broken by a huge, hard, bumpy rock.

OUCH, thought Edwin as he got to his feet. He felt bruised. Bruised, and very, very hot.

He looked around. The rock they were standing on was bobbing in a boiling lake of red-hot lava.

All around the bubbling lake was a circular cliff.

They had fallen into the mouth of a volcano.

"Well, at least things can't get any worse," said Minister Jill, three seconds before things did.

Glowing orange shapes bounced from rock to rock, squirting streams of fire at the adventurers.

"Fire toads!" gasped Megan.

King Edwin once read about those in a book called *Deadly Beasts and Where to Avoid Them, Unless You Really Want to Find Them, But If You Do You're Daft in the Head.*

Fire toads live in volcanos, swim in lava, and breathe jets of sticky molten fire everywhere. Because they glow in the dark,

they make handy bedside
night-lights, as long as
you don't mind your
night-light roasting off
your face halfway through your
bedtime story.

But the main thing anyone needs to know
about fire toads is—don't get trapped in a
volcano with hundreds of them.

"Okay, here's what we do!" said Edwin.

The others looked at him.

I have no idea what we should do, thought
Edwin. *So I'd better think of something quickly
or I'm going to feel very stupid . . .*

Hunt the Voolith

Emperor Nurbison rode south. Even though there was loads of room on his massive horse, he made Globulus run alongside.

"Ha! Those foolish fools are so foolish! It was so easy to fool them. Because of their foolishness," said the emperor.

Globulus guessed the emperor had just
read up on *fool* in *Cool Words for Evil Rulers
to Use.*

"It was, like, you know, very clever and stuff, Your Greatness. Losing the joust. On purpose and everything," said Globulus.

"Indeed!" said Nurbison. "I couldn't ever win with that stupid lance or that ridiculous helmet. I wanted King Edwin out of the way—and with that map, he'll be out of the way forever! If I'd just handed it to him, he would have known something was wrong with it. I had to make him think I didn't want him to have it.

FOO HOO HOO HOO HOO!"

"But, Your Stunningness, it, errr . . . it must've been really, really, really embarrassing, losing the joust. Even though you meant to. 'Cause you hate to lose, yeah? I mean, you totally don't like it."

Emperor Nurbison didn't reply. He just clenched his teeth and gripped the horse's reins a little tighter.

"'Cause you was all, kind of, down in the mud, sort of thing," said Globulus. "Arms and legs in the air. Everybody laughing, all of that."

Still no reply.

"All them peasants cheering for King Edwin, it must have been—"

"SILENCE, WORM!" shouted the emperor. "Edwin's gone, and that's what matters! Now he can't get between me and the Voolith. And I have plans for the Voolith, oh yes. I have plans."

The emperor tugged on the reins, and the black horse stopped. Before them was a towering pillar of jagged rock.

"That, unless I am mistaken—and I am never mistaken—is the tallest lump of rock in this whole miserable wilderness," said the emperor. "Climb it, Globulus, then look around with the telescope and spot the Voolith. I'll stay down here and practice my evil yoga."

Emperor Nurbison bent his body into all kinds of evil yoga shapes. It helped the

ALIEN WARLORD

FURIOUS GOBLIN

WIZARD OF
BENDY HARSHNESS

MAN-EATING
PLANT

emperor focus his evil thoughts. Also, it was very good for his back.

Globulus clambered up the rocky tower, stopping now and again for a rest and to fight off the vultures trying to peck out his eyes and brain.

Once he was at the top, he popped the telescope open and took a long, slow look around the whole horizon.

He looked east.

He looked south.

He looked **west.**

He lowered the telescope and thought it over.

He looked east again. Then he scrambled

down the rock as fast as he could

to tell the emperor.

A couple of hours later, Emperor
Nurbison and Globulus were crouched behind
a bush. Ahead of them was a forest clearing,
and asleep in the clearing,

the Voolith.

It was enormous. Even bigger than everybody said it was. It didn't have nine hundred and twenty-seven and a half eyes, or even fifty, but it certainly had more eyes than any creature needed. As it snored, its awesome teeth scraped against one another. And it stank of meat, because it had been noshing on sheep and goats and deer and wolves and bears and badgers all day.

"Now, Globulus, what do you suppose I intend to do with this Voolith?" whispered the emperor.

"Well, I don't reckon you'll, like, just fight it like you told everyone. 'Cause you're totally all about the sneaky plans and that. So . . . something else."

"Correct, Globulus. I'm going to do

something much more clever. Because I'm the cleverest. If anybody else tells you they are the cleverest, tell them I am the cleverester. And before you say it, *cleverester* is a word, because I say it is, and I'm an emperor."

The emperor reached in his big saddlebag and pulled out two paper lanterns and five megaphones.

"I'm going to become that creature's master. And how do you imagine I will do that?" asked the emperor.

"Errrrr—win its trust?" said Globulus.

"Become its friend, yeah? Like, train it, so it loves you and never leaves your side, type of thing."

"Globulus, you are such a baby!" chuckled the emperor. "I

can't be bothered with all that. It would take ages. No, I'm just going to become an even bigger monster and show the Voolith who's boss."

Globulus knew the emperor was a master of disguise. The hermit costume was brilliant, even though being the hump had been a squeeze and his chin still hadn't quite gone back to its old shape. But he just couldn't see how the emperor could become a giant monster.

"We wait till nightfall," said Emperor Nurbison.

When it was dark, the Voolith was awoken by a deafening bellow from inside the bushes.

"YOU! YES, YOU, VOOLITH! FEAR ME!

FOR I AM THE GREATEST MONSTER IN

THE WORLD! RRRRRAAAAARRRRRR!"

In the darkness of the trees, unseen by

the monster, stood Emperor Nurbison. He was

shouting into a megaphone, and the sound
from that went into another megaphone, then
another, then two more.

It was a mega-mega-mega-mega-megaphone,
and it made his voice incredibly loud.

The Voolith snarled, drooling from its saberlike teeth. It was ready to pounce.

"OH, YOU WANT TO FIGHT ME, DO YOU?" boomed Nurbison. "DON'T YOU REALIZE HOW ENORMOUS I AM?"

Two glowing eyes appeared in the gloomy forest. They were huge and very far apart.

It was really the emperor and Globulus, holding up two paper lanterns on long poles, but the Voolith didn't know that. To the Voolith, this looked like the eyes of a colossal new creature with a head as big as a barn.

The Voolith whimpered and backed away. For the first time in its life, it had met something huger and scarier than itself.

"YES, BE AFRAID!" said the voice from the darkness. "BOW DOWN AND CLOSE YOUR EYES. FOR I AM NOW YOUR MASTER! AND I'M TAKING YOU ON A JOURNEY, VOOLITH. A JOURNEY . . . TO EDWINLAND!"

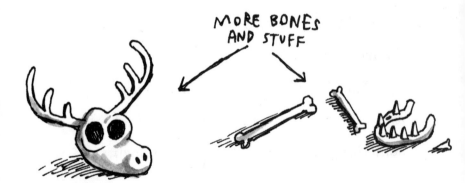

MORE BONES AND STUFF

Edwin Has an Idea

Edwin had an idea.

Good thing, too, because he was trapped deep in the crater of a volcano with his friends, surrounded by deadly flame-gushing fire toads.

"Open the candy sacks!"
said Edwin. "Get the chewy red
licorice twists!"

They all ripped sacks open, gathering
the licorice together while they ducked blasts
from the fire toads.

"Tie the licorice together into one long
rope," said Edwin. "I'll protect you from the
fire toads."

While Megan and Jill wove the candy
together into one long licorice
rope, Edwin jumped

back and forth, flicking toads into the lava with his sword and stopping

their fiery blasts with his shield. One of his eyebrows got toasted off, so he paused for a second to draw it back on with a felt-tip pen.

When the red licorice rope was long enough, Megan held one end of it in the breath of a fire toad to make it gooey, then hurled that end as high as she could.

The gooey bit stuck fast to the volcano's rim. They had a way out.

Megan climbed the rope first, carrying Colin. Jill clambered up second. Edwin swatted toads away left, right, and center.

127

CHEW
GULP
NOSH
NOSH
CHEW

Edwin went up last.
This was partly because he
knew heroes always get their
friends out of danger first.
And partly because, if he
went last, he could eat the
rope as he climbed.

Once they had hauled
themselves out of the
volcano and stumbled
from the mist,
the adventurers
flopped down on
the ground and
tried to figure
out what had
just happened.

"Does the Voolith really live down there?" said Edwin, frowning at his crown. The heat had made the pointy bits go all droopy.

"Maybe," said Minister Jill. "But something feels wrong about all this. Pass me the map."

Minister Jill unfolded the map and found the area that said VOOLITH'S LAIR. She scraped at it with her thumbnail.

Chips of paint flaked away. Soon she could see the writing underneath.

EVERLASTING MIG

VOLCANO OF TOADY DOOM

FLAKE FLAKE

SCRAPE SCRAPE

"So that's it!" said Jill. "Emperor Nurbison wanted you to win the joust so you would get this map. He changed it with paint and ink. And he rolled a wet tea bag over the new part to make it look old."

said Edwin, slamming his fist against his knee, then pretending his knee didn't hurt. *Bottybag* was the rudest word Edwin knew, and he didn't use it often.

"All so we would meet our doom in the volcano, and he could find the Voolith," said Jill.

"But he said he'd be a hero," said Megan. "Don't get me wrong, I still think he's the most evil person in the universe. But it would be a good thing if he did defeat the monster."

"Nurbison doesn't care about being a hero," said Jill. "I suspect he has a really sneaky plan for the Voolith . . ."

"I should have seen this coming," said Edwin. "I kind-of-sort-of saw him do an evil smile after the joust, and stroke his beard and pump his fist. But I forgot to tell you both. Please don't be angry with me."

After a very long pause, Jill said, "Edwin, I'm not angry with you."

"She is a little bit angry," Megan whispered in Edwin's ear.

"Yeah, I know," Edwin whispered back.

"We **have** to get back to Edwinland right now!" said Jill. "I fear it's in terrible, terrible danger."

"But it took us five days to get from Edwinland to here," said Megan.

It was true. Edwinland was far, far away.

Colin stepped forward.

"Neigh," said Colin.

He was speaking horse language, and what he meant by this *neigh* was:

GOOD FRIENDS, CLIMB UPON MY BACK. I AM BUT A TINY HORSE, BUT I HAVE THE HEART OF A MIGHTY STALLION. I SHALL RIDE FASTER THAN THE CLOUD-SWEEPING WIND, SWIFTER YET THAN ANY ARROW. EVERY LOYAL HORSE WISHES FOR ONE GREAT RIDE IN HIS LIFE, AND THIS IS MINE. I SHALL NOT FAIL YOU. CLIMB UPON MY BACK, MY FRIENDS, AND I SHALL BEAR YOU HOME.

None of them understood what he was saying, so Colin held a stick between his teeth and drew a picture in the sand.

Then they understood. They climbed upon his back, and that tiny horse galloped like he had never galloped before.

I just hope we get to Edwinland in time, thought Edwin.

So it was "mig" and not "fost," thought Megan.

Thump...Thump... Thump...

In Edwinland, the peasants were very excited. King Edwin and his loyal friends Jill, Megan, and Colin were sure to return sometime soon, having chased away the terrifying Voolith. Heroes deserve a heroes' welcome, so that's what the peasants would give them.

They made an
enormous cake
full of cream and
chocolate and
jam. And no
vegetables. With
Jill away, there
was nobody
to make
them have
their fifty
portions a day,
so vegetable eating had slipped a bit. The
fields were full of huge uneaten pumpkins
and squashes. When everything was ready,
the peasants heard a distant THUMP . . .
THUMP . . . THUMP . . . sound.

"That's them coming now!" said one peasant. "Places, everyone!"

The peasants ran to the village green.

Baxter the Hermit stood on a wooden platform, ready to give the four adventurers their medals while crying a single tear.

A small girl named Natasha put up her hand.

"Something's wrong. Those are very, very loud footsteps," she said.

THUMP . . .

THUMP . . .
THUMP . . .

The noise was getting louder by the moment.

"I can't wait to hear about all their thrilling exploits!" said a peasant.

"I still think those footsteps are very heavy," said Natasha.

THUMP . . .
THUMP . . .
THUMP . . .

Now the ground shook a little with each *thump*. The water in the village pond rippled.

"If those are King Edwin's footsteps," said another peasant, "they seem a little bit loud. And heavy."

"Which is what I've been saying," said Natasha.

"Oh, I know what that is!" said a third peasant. "Young Edwin must have had a growth spurt."

"That'll be it," said the first peasant.

Everybody got ready to shout "Hooray!"— except Natasha, who hid inside a barrel.

THUMP . . .

THUMP . . .

THUMP . . .

And around the side of the great mountain of Hetherang-Dundister-Underploshy-Smeltus came the monster.

The Voolith carried a huge net full of rocks on its back. Perched high on the rocks was Emperor Nurbison, steering the monster with long reins and bellowing through the mega-mega-mega-mega-megaphone.

"I AM THE NURBISONSTER! THE MIGHTIEST MONSTER IN THE WORLD!

I AM RIDING MY SLAVE, THE VOOLITH,
TO EDWINLAND. VOOLITH? CRUSH THIS
KINGDOM! DESTROY EVERYTHING! FOO
HOO HOO HOO!"

The Voolith couldn't see that it wasn't a
monster on his back, just a tiny little man.
Even though it had dozens of eyes, none of
them were on the back of its head.

Nurbison twitched the reins, and the
Voolith thundered toward Village, grabbing
sheep and cows from the fields and hurling
them into its huge mouth.

"Guards? Charge!" shouted
Centurion Alisha.

The palace guards sprinted toward the
monster, swords drawn. But one swipe from the
monster's great clawed foot sent them flying—

sPLOOSH—into the village pond.

"WHERE IS YOUR KING TO SAVE YOU?" boomed Nurbison. "HE HAS PERISHED—AS EDWINLAND SHALL PERISH! THEN HIS NAME WILL BE FORGOTTEN FOR ETERNITY! AND IF YOU DON'T KNOW WHAT *ETERNITY* MEANS BECAUSE YOU'RE AN IGNORANT PEASANT, IT MEANS *FOREVER*!"

"Shall no one save us?" wailed the peasants.

"I will!" called a voice.

King Edwin's voice.

Colin hurtled into Village with Edwin and his friends on his back.

The little horse plowed up half the village green as he skidded to a halt.

This was Edwin's moment to face the Voolith in single combat, so Jill and Megan jumped off.

"It's my destiny," said Edwin. "All my life has prepared me for this hour. With just this sword and shield, I . . . I . . . I'd better stop making a big speech and just get on with it, shouldn't I, Jill?"

"Good idea," said Jill.

"Colin? Charge!" said Edwin.

Colin keeled over, gasping and panting.

Well, he has run quite a long way today, thought Edwin, patting Colin's nose.

So the brave nine-year-old warrior ran at the Voolith.

All on his own.

"Flashypants wahooo-waaaa!"

"CURSE YOU, BOY, FOR NOT PERISHING AS I WISHED YOU TO PERISH!" said the emperor, who had read the word *perish* in his book that afternoon.

King Edwin smashed his sword down on the monster's huge, dirty toenail.

The sword SHATTERED.

A tug on the reins from Nurbison, and the Voolith booted King Edwin, hard.

The boy flew high over the town and landed—*skuh-plomp!*—in a huge overripe pumpkin in the vegetable fields.

A great **"FOO HOO HOO HOOOOOO"** echoed over Edwinland.

The emperor steered the Voolith to the main street and made it stomp—one by one—on every candy shop in Village.

Every single one.

Now Edwin was really angry.

The Windmill of Even Worse Nightmares

Emperor Nurbison was having a fantastic day, sitting on top of a monster and making it stomp all over the kingdom of his worst enemy. King Edwin might have survived the volcano and the fire toads, but it didn't matter. The boy was no match for the Voolith.

I like having a terrifying giant monster as a pet, thought the emperor as the Voolith punched Megan's favorite bakery into rubble. *If I find another, I can breed them, and cut their hair into funny shapes for a laugh. Like poodles. Huge town-trampling, cow-gobbling poodles.*

The emperor looked around for a really big building to smash.

The tallest thing in Village was a windmill. Not a small model like on the emperor's mini-golf course, but a huge one for grinding wheat.

A windmill, thought the emperor. *I don't like windmills.*

"HALT! TURN! DEMOLISH!" the emperor bellowed in the Voolith's ear with the mega-mega-mega-mega-megaphone.

The beast lumbered toward the mill.

SQUELCH!

The spinning sails of the windmill jabbed the Voolith in the eye. It had so many eyes that it was bound to happen.

"JUNZZAAARRRR!"

the creature howled, which in Voolith

language means, "Ouch, I am badly hurt in

my twenty-third eye."

The creature spun around,

clutching its face.

The sails of the windmill were still

spinning.

A sail knocked Emperor Nurbison off

his perch.

When the Voolith opened its eyes again, there was a small figure far below on the ground, clutching the mega-mega-mega-mega-megaphone.

"YOU! VOOLITH!"

The emperor threw Globulus at the monster to get its attention. Globulus bounced off its belly.

"YES, I'M DOWN HERE! NOW PUT ME UP ON YOUR BACK. AT ONCE!"

The monster blinked and studied Nurbison. A Voolith is not the cleverest of creatures, but as the emperor raged and spluttered, it gradually figured something out. It hadn't really been carrying another monster on its back. That big voice came from a human.

Just a teeny tiny human.

"MUUZZZONNDARR!"

raged the Voolith as it shook the net of rocks off its shoulders.

It scooped the emperor up with one great claw and tossed him into its gaping mouth.

Gulp!

And the mighty Nurbisonster was

swallowed by the Voolith.

wailed Globulus.

"MMMMMMM," hummed the Voolith. It knew all about eating animals, but it had never tried human before. And human tasted nice. Like deer, but without those pesky antlers, which got stuck in the gums.

The Voolith wanted another human for dessert.

It saw King Edwin Flashypants, clambering out of the gooey smashed pumpkin.

THUMP . . .

THUMP . . .

THUMP!

The monster bounded to the vegetable patches, snatched up the goo-covered King Edwin, and flung him into its mouth.

Inside the Voolith's mouth, King Edwin backed up against a giant tooth. The monster's tongue slimed toward him like a wet hippo.

I'm doomed, thought Edwin. *But I've been doomed before and that didn't stop me. A hero never gives up.*

He punched the monster's tongue.
Mashed-up pumpkin flew off him and landed
all over the creature's taste buds. The tongue
wriggled like it was in pain, then came at
him again—and this time, Edwin kicked it.

More pumpkin sprayed around. The tongue slid to the other side of the mouth, flapping in agony.

Aha! thought Edwin. *I get it. The monster likes meaty things, like goats and sheep and emperors . . .*

And it doesn't like vegetables.

It's just like me!

So if I give it the most vegetably taste it's ever tasted . . .

King Edwin dived onto the tongue, rolling around and splatting pumpkin mash all over the big wet thing.

The Voolith **coughed**

and spluttered

and SPAT Edwin right out . . .

AAAAAAHHHHH

. . . and Megan caught him.

"Listen, everyone!" said the king from Megan's arms. "It doesn't like vegetables, so that's what we'll fight it with! Quickly, to the fields!"

Everybody ran to the vegetable patches. The palace guards cut arm holes, leg holes, and face holes in the big squashes and pumpkins. The Voolith would never touch anyone wearing those.

Safe in their new armor, the peasants, the palace guards, Edwin, Jill, Megan, and Baxter launched an all-out vegetable attack. They catapulted tomatoes and cabbages. They used bows to shoot leeks and cucumbers like arrows.

Even Globulus helped.

"Voolith! I will, like, you know, totally take my revenge on you, type of thing!" cried Globulus.

Soon the creature was plastered head to toe with squished-up veggies. For a Voolith, this was the most revolting thing in the world.

"VUNGGAARRNUU! GWERREEE! YARRRBB!"

it howled as turnips pinged off its eyes and a big ripe squash burst on its nose.

It was all too much for the monster. It wobbled, then fainted, crashing to the ground like a toppled factory chimney—if the chimney were made of teeth, hair, and eyes.

The Voolith was defeated.

"But, you know, ummm . . . what about the emperor?" said Globulus.

11.

The Belly of the Beast

Alisha ran up to Minister Jill and saluted so hard that she dented her own helmet.

"Minister, we've lost some buildings and sheep and cows, but the only casualty is Emperor Nurbison."

"Our deadliest foe, gobbled up by the monster he failed to control," said the minister. "What a terrible shame! How very sad. Never mind."

"Maybe I can climb inside the Voolith," said King Edwin. "Go in through its nose, see if I can find the emperor."

"Your Majesty," said Jill, "I must remind you that he's massively evil and wants to destroy you and your kingdom. Annoying, I know, but there it is."

"You're right, Jill," said Edwin. "But still: if there's a chance of saving him, I've got to try . . ." King Edwin cleared his throat, which meant he wanted everyone to listen to what he said next.

Megan scribbled that down. It was going to sound great in her heroic song.

"All right," said Jill. "But first, let's make another one of those chewy red licorice ropes. You'll see why."

Soon, King Edwin was squeezing into
the creature's nostril, pulling himself along
by its nose hairs.

Lighting his way with some fireflies in
a jar, Edwin squirmed through yucky slimy
tubes. He didn't know for sure where the
stomach was, but he reckoned that as long as
he followed the smell of meat, he'd get there.

One last squeeze, and Edwin stood at
the end of a tube, looking into a great
chamber made of wobbly flesh.
Below was a lake of steaming acid,
with cow and sheep bones
sticking out of it.

Yes, this was the stomach all right.

"Help! Help!" said a weak, scared voice.

High above
the acid pit,
dangling from
a droopy bit of
flesh, was Emperor
Nurbison.

"Emperor!" said
King Edwin. "If I get
you out of here, do you promise never to do
anything bad to me or my kingdom again?"

"Yes!" whimpered the emperor.

"Do you swear? On your beautifully
shiny beard?"

Edwin knew
you have to
swear on
something

very important to you, and Nurbison had a pretty high opinion of his facial hair.

"I swear!" spluttered the emperor.

"Then swing on that droopy thing, and get ready to grab my hand!" said Edwin.

The emperor swung back and forth, getting higher and higher each time. One slip, and he would fall into the lake of acid far below.

"Now, grab!" said the young king.

Emperor Nurbison grabbed Edwin's outstretched arm . . . and the king pulled him to safety.

"You okay?" asked Edwin.

"I am more than okay," said the emperor, straightening up and smiling. "But as for you . . ."

And the emperor kicked Edwin over the ledge.

"FOO HOO HOO HOO!"

cackled the evil emperor as Edwin plummeted
toward the deadly acid.

"That's peculiar," said the emperor as
he watched the king fall. "He's tied to a rope
made of chewy red licorice."

Outside, by the head of the still-sleeping
Voolith, Jill watched the other end of the
red licorice rope racing into the creature's
nostril.

"The king is falling! Quick, pull the
rope!" she said.

Jill, Megan, Alisha, and Globulus grabbed
the rope and ran away from the monster.
Globulus was so short that his feet didn't
touch the ground. But he was pedaling them
very fast in the air. Maybe that helped a bit.

Inside the Voolith's belly, the rope jerked
tight, just before Edwin plopped into the
stomach acid.

Then the rope pulled him back up again very, VERY fast.

BANG!

Edwin smacked into Nurbison's boots, knocking the emperor right off his feet.

Edwin was hauled back through the gloopy tubes . . .

. . . but evil Emperor Nurbison plummeted

down,

down into the belly of

the Voolith.

Edwin shot from the Voolith's nostril with a loud **vuH–PLOOMP**.

Everybody gathered around as the king told them what had happened.

"I don't think we'll see Emperor Nurbison again," said the king sadly.

Everyone was silent for a moment.

Globulus sniveled.

Everyone who had a hat took it off.

Those who didn't have hats ran to the hat shop to buy hats just to take off. But they discovered that all the hats had been sold when people were buying them to throw into the air in Chapter One.

"Oh, he might still make it," said Natasha, peeping out from her barrel. "The Voolith had plenty to eat today. If it needs to go to the loo soon, then Emperor Nurbison might pop out the other end before he gets digested."

It was true. The Voolith had eaten lots and lots of animals.

There was a low rumbling noise.

"Earthquake!" said Megan. "Everyone hang on to something!" The nearest thing to her was Jill's nose, so Megan held tight to that.

"Sounded very wet and squishy for an earthquake," said Jill. "Also, please let go of my nose. It's making my voice sound weird."

Another rumble—louder this time. The Voolith's belly wobbled and twitched.

"Told you," said Natasha as she pulled the barrel over her head and scuttled away.

"Everybody take cover!" yelled Minister Jill. "I think the Voolith's about to—"

It took a couple of minutes for stinky blobs of Voolith poo to stop raining down from the sky.

Inside the very biggest pile of horrible stuff, something was moving. A blob oozed out and rolled to the ground. Then arms and legs emerged.

The reeking lump struggled to its feet. Everybody backed away holding their noses—apart from Globulus, who handed the blob a tall black crown.

"Globulus? I think I'd like to go home now, please," said Emperor Nurbison quietly.

What We've All Learned

They had to get rid of the Voolith before it woke up. The peasants built a big raft with logs, rolled the creature onto it, then pushed the raft out to sea.

Edwin and Jill stood on a cliff, watching the snoring beast drift away on the tide.

"The Voolith isn't evil like Nurbison,"
said Edwin. "Stomping around and eating
things is the only way it knows how to live.
Hey! Maybe the raft will wash up on some
kind of Voolith island, where there's loads of
them, and it can have friends and be happy."

"Yes, maybe," said Minister Jill.

She knew it would probably wash up on the beach of some other kingdom, like Clab or Ickum Bokum. But when it did, it would definitely be somebody else's problem and not hers.

After every adventure, the king, his friends, and his subjects liked to sit on the village green to talk about what they had all learned.

So that's just what they did.

One of the peasants stood up.

"We've learned our king is brave and bold. He's as good as any grown-up king!" she said.

King Edwin stood up.

"Ah, but I'll tell you what I've learned," said the king. "I've learned just how much I need you all. I thought I could be the big hero and beat the monster by myself—but in the end, it took every one of us to do it."

Everybody cheered that.

"I also learned vegetables are cool," said Edwin. "They're terrific for throwing at Vooliths, anyway. But I'm really sorry, Minister Jill—I don't know if I can eat fifty of them a day."

Minister Jill stood up. "The truth is— nobody really needs fifty a day," she said.

Every eyebrow in Village went up at the same time. Even Edwin's felt-tip one.

"Five portions is about right," said Jill. "But if I said five, you might eat only one, or even none. So I thought if I told you fifty, you might eat five. I'm really sorry."

"It's okay. You just wanted us to be healthy," said King Edwin. "If five is what we need, let's all promise to eat five portions of vegetables every single day!"

"We promise!" the crowd shouted.
And from that moment on, they all ate five portions every day, and enjoyed them, too.

Megan stood up.

"I've learned loads of stuff, probably!" she said.

Baxter the Hermit stood up.

"I've learned it's more fun to live here than all alone in a house of dead wasps. I think I'll stay in Edwinland."

Nobody was sure what to think about that.

Then Baxter said,

Now they knew that for sure, everyone
was very happy for Baxter to stay.

Colin stood up.

NEIGH

said Colin.

"I reckon Colin said, 'I have learned the bonds of our friendship shall never be broken!' Or something noble like that," said Edwin.

What Colin really said was, PLEASE DON'T PUT ME THROUGH THAT EVER AGAIN.

Now that they had all learned, they needed to rebuild Village. But that could wait till tomorrow. First, it was time for a party.

They all ate big slices of the cake the peasants had made for Edwin—but with lots of vegetables, too. Baxter hung the medals around the heroes' necks. There was dancing and games to play—but best of all was Megan the Jester's song about their great adventure.

Long into the night,

everybody listened spellbound

as Megan sang of King Edwin,

the joust, the slight

dampness,

the volcano, the Great Ride of Colin the

Horse, how they beat the Voolith with

vegetables, how Emperor Nurbison got

covered in stuff you just don't want to get

covered in, and how they couldn't get his cloak clean so they had to send him home in Megan's spare pajamas with the pink teddy bear pattern.

"Edwin, I'm very proud of you," said Minister Jill when Megan's song was over. "One reason is because you always keep your promises."

"Thanks, Jill!" said King Edwin, who was fairly sure she was building up to something.

"So, I bet you'll promise to have no more scary adventures, won't you?" said Jill.

"Ooh, look over there—fireworks!" said Edwin, quickly stepping away.

Well, it was worth a try, thought Jill, smiling.

Meanwhile, far away in Nurbisonia, by the roaring gray sea, there stood a dark cottage.

In the cottage was a dark cupboard.

And in the dark cupboard was a doll.

Was it an ordinary doll?

No. It was not.

Was it a

MAGICAL

doll?

Yes. It was very much one of those.

But magical how?

We will find out.

In another book.

The Amazing Adventures of EMPEROR NURBISON'S TWO-HEADED RAT

ANDY RILEY has done lots of funny writing for film and TV, and he's even won prizes for it, like BAFTAs and an Emmy. For TV, Andy cowrote the scripts for David Walliams's *Gangsta Granny* and *The Boy in the Dress*, and *Robbie the Reindeer*. The films he's written for include *Gnomeo and Juliet* and *The Pirates! In an Adventure with Scientists!* Andy really loves cowboy hats, and he can do a brilliant "FOO HOO HOO."